Toucan Do It!

By Alix & Ryan Ciovacco

For our son, Mac:

May you always believe that you can do anything you put your mind to.

You can *(Tou-can)* do it!

Toucan Toby and his friends gather each morning before school. Everyone flies to school together except for Toby, who doesn't know how to fly.

Toby is sad because he can't fly with his friends and must walk the long way with his teacher, Demi the Donkey.

"Don't be sad, Toby. You are a toucan and toucans can't fly," says Demi. Toby wishes he can fly like all the other birds, so he decides to teach himself by copying his other friends.

Baby ducks learn how to fly by jumping off a cliff over water.

So Toby follows Dottie the Duck as she jumps off the cliff and begins to fly...

...but Toby crashes into the water below.

Baby geese learn how to fly by taking a long running start and then jumping into the air.

So Toby follows Iza the Goose as she runs and jumps into the air...

...but Toby crashes into a rock.

Baby bats learn how to fly by hanging upside down and dropping from a branch.

So Toby hangs upside down and then drops like Bibi the Bat as he begins to fly...

...but Toby crashes to the ground.

Toucan Toby watches an airplane flying in the sky and gets an idea.

He ties a branch to his wings and jumps off the cliff into the air...

...but again, Toby crashes into the water below.

Sad and wet, Toby meets Earl the Owl and tells him about his failure to fly like his friends. Earl says, "Don't try to fly like your friends. Fly like Toby. TOUCAN DO IT, TOBY!"

With his eyes closed, Toby jumps off the branch and begins flapping his wings...

...and when Toby opens his eyes, he is flying high in the sky!

Now Toby can fly with his friends to school every day, and he is a happy toucan once again!

The End!

Made in the USA
Middletown, DE
14 August 2018